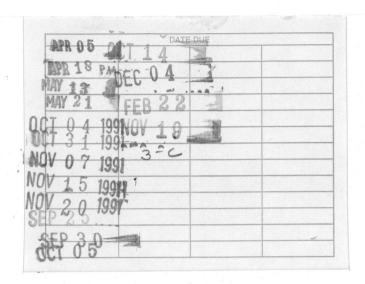

DATE DUE

APR 05 OCT 14		
APR 18 PM DEC 04		
MAY 13		
MAY 21 FEB 22		
OCT 04 199 NOV 10		
OCT 31 1991 3-C		
NOV 07 1991		
NOV 15 1991		
NOV 20 1991		
SEP 23		
SEP 30		
OCT 05		

E
GLA

Glass, Marvin.

What happened today,
Freddy Groundhog?

837967 01101   05036C

What Happened Today, Freddy Groundhog?

Marvin Glass

Crown Publishers, Inc., New York

Published by Crown Publishers, Inc., 225 Park Avenue
South, New York, New York 10003 and represented in
Canada by the Canadian MANDA Group.
CROWN is a trademark of Crown Publishers, Inc.
Manufactured in Hong Kong

Library of Congress Cataloging-in-Publication Data
Glass, Marvin.
        What happened today, Freddy Groundhog?/by Marvin
Glass.
        Summary: As February 2 approaches, Freddy
Groundhog gets ready for the big event on Groundhog Day.
        [1. Woodchuck—Fiction.   2. Groundhog Day—
Fiction.]   I. Title.
PZ7.G48124Wh 1989
[E]—dc19

ISBN 0-517-57140-4

10 9 8 7 6 5 4 3 2 1

First Edition

All summer long, Freddy the groundhog just lazed about, growing chubby, eating all the leaves and grass he could get ahold of.

Now the days were getting shorter, winter was coming, and something was stirring under the ground.

"Come on in," called his father.

"It's time to get ready for a good hi-ber-nation. I mean sleepy time!" his father said.

"Wigglin' woodchucks, that sounds great!" said Freddy.

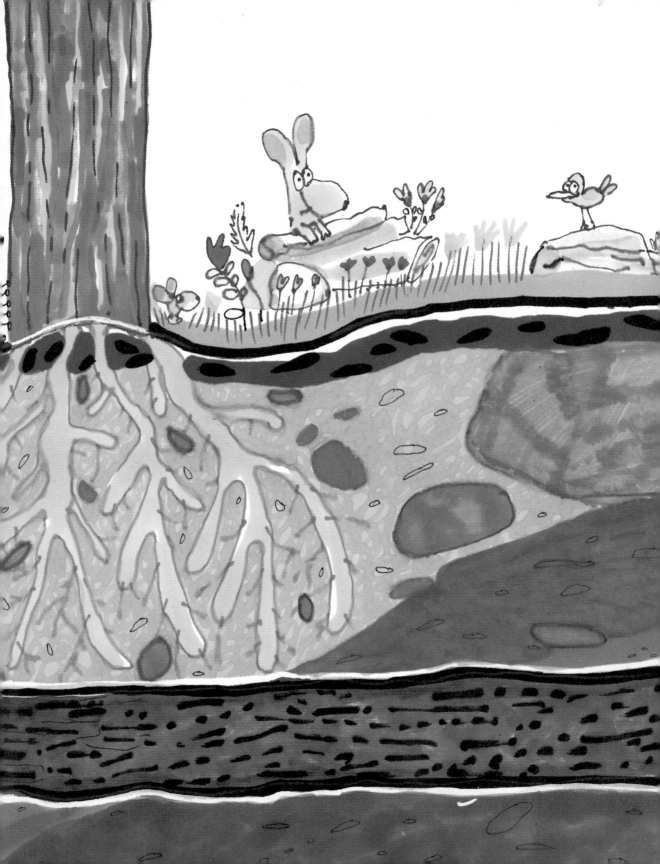

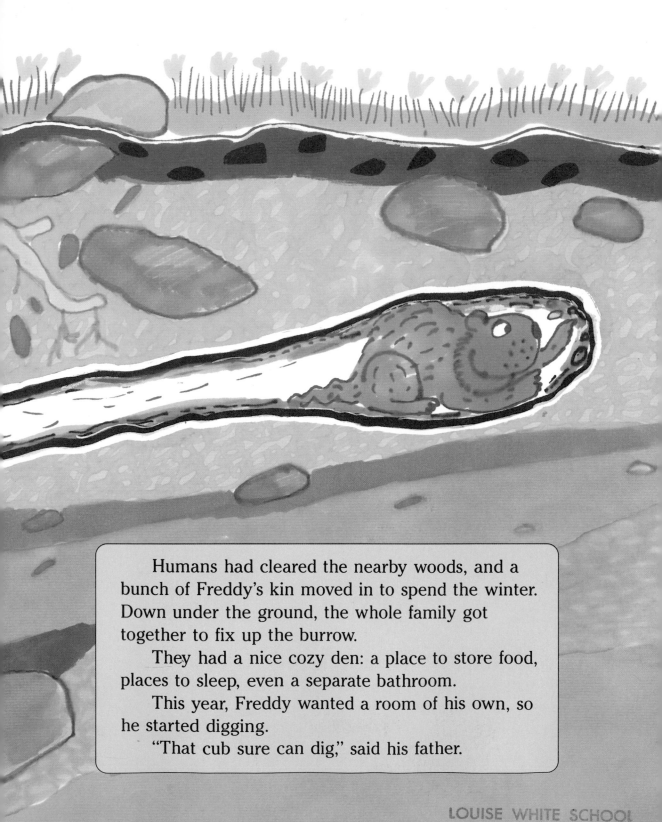

Humans had cleared the nearby woods, and a bunch of Freddy's kin moved in to spend the winter. Down under the ground, the whole family got together to fix up the burrow.

They had a nice cozy den: a place to store food, places to sleep, even a separate bathroom.

This year, Freddy wanted a room of his own, so he started digging.

"That cub sure can dig," said his father.

Freddy dug under the woods. He dug under the fields. Then he dug under Farmer Green's barnyard.

Suddenly, Freddy felt a heavy crunch. Charlie the horse stepped right on top of the tunnel and nearly broke a leg.

Farmer Green hollered, "Wait till I get my hands on that *low-down* groundhog!"

"Chucks," said Freddy.

Digging as fast as he could, Freddy plowed right into Doris Chipmunk's hideout.

"Get out of here, you *low-down* groundhog!" she screeched. "Can't an animal have any privacy anymore?"

"Aw, chucks," said Freddy. "I didn't mean to do it." Doris was the one chipmunk he wanted to be friends with.

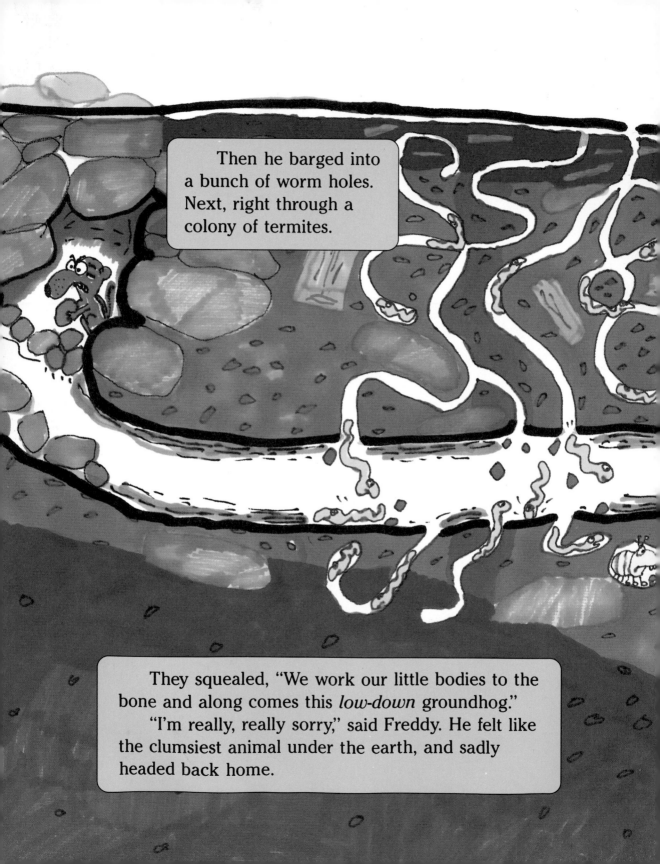

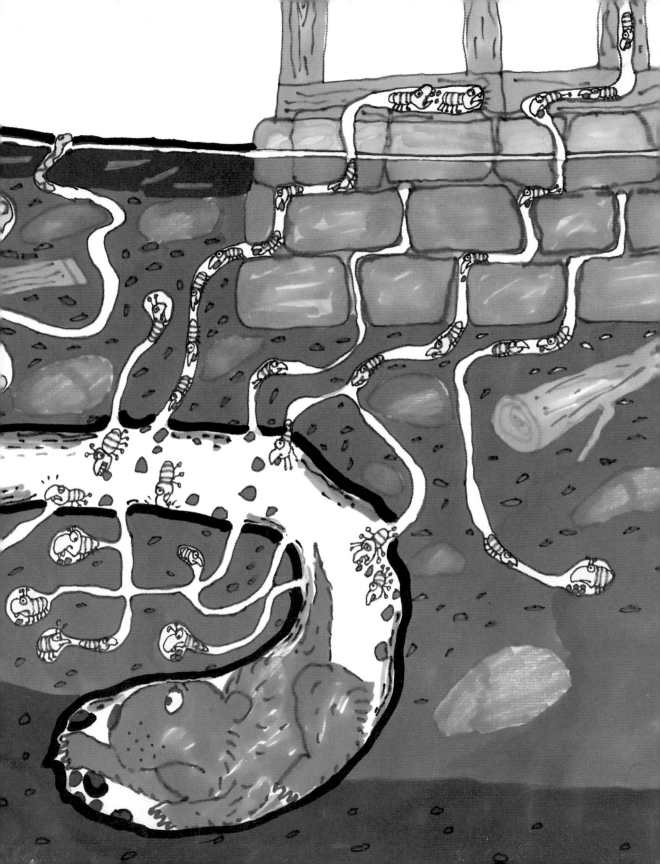

Freddy was surprised to see his father and mother helping make up his bed. Even his sister Gertie brought him a soft grass pillow.

"You've got to get a good winter's rest, Fred," said his mother.

"...Because," said his father, "this year it's your turn to have a BIG DAY!"

Freddy's dad told him about the curious ideas the humans had. Every February 2 they all wait around for a groundhog to come out of his hole and look for his shadow. If he sees it, they figure there'll be six more weeks of winter.

"That's *amazing*," said Freddy. His mother smiled.

Freddy curled up in bed, wondering whether anyone would really make a fuss about a *low-down* groundhog like himself.

"Chucks! If only I could come out as a famous ballplayer. Maybe shortstop on the Hometown Beavers.

Even Doris Chipmunk would perk up.

"Or better still, a famous astronaut, zipping through space even faster than Jerry the squirrel.

"But that could never be," Freddy thought. "I'm doomed to crawl around under the earth, just a *low-down* groundhog.

"Chucks," said Freddy sadly, as he fell asleep.

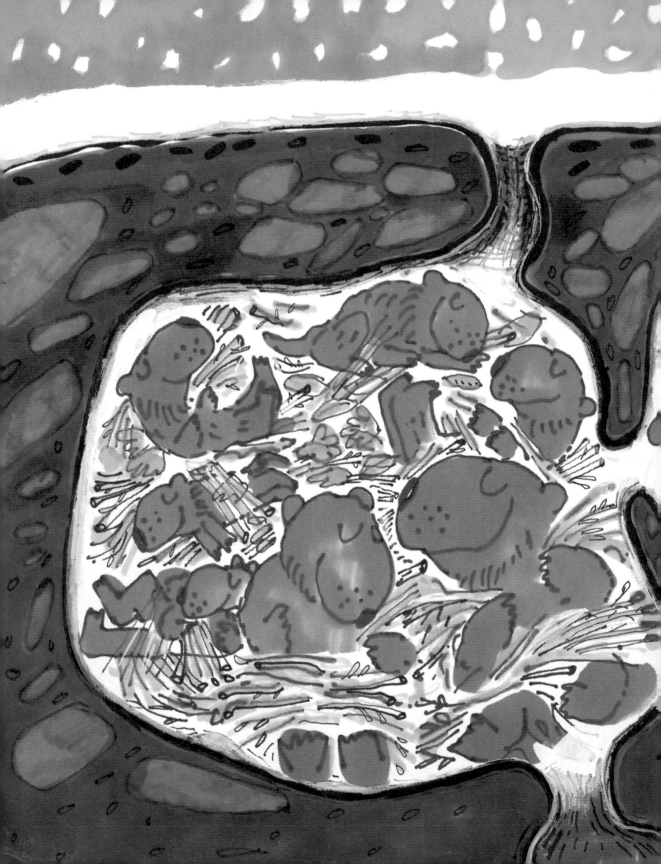

And that's what the whole family did—sleep...
all through the winter.
It was hibernation time.

He looked a bit thin, but his mother said, "No matter."

Freddy dug his way back to Farmer Green's pasture, where he planned to come out. He was careful not to barge into anybody this time.

The closer he got, the better he could hear the crowd of humans stomping about in the snow. And there was Farmer Green having his say, as usual.

Fred worked up enough courage to make his entrance. He inched his way out of the tunnel and looked around.

"What if I can't find my shadow?" Freddy thought. "What if I'm really a *low-down* groundhog just like everybody says?"

He looked all over—but his shadow wasn't there!

Just then, Farmer Green burst into a grin and a holler.

"WhoooooOOOO-ie!" he shouted. "This here groundhog can't find its shadow. That means we're going to have an early spring. This sure is a *heads-up* groundhog! This sure is a BIG DAY!"

Freddy didn't know what to make of it. "First he calls me *low down*, now he says I'm *heads up*," Freddy thought. "Chucks! I'm just glad to be a plain and simple groundhog."

That evening, the whole family came out to see him on TV. Doris Chipmunk came along, too.

Back home, Freddy turned to his sister. "Study up, Gertie. Next year it's your turn to have a BIG DAY."

"Chucks!" said Gertie.

And they all went back to sleep.